The Wriggly, Wriggly Baby

By Jessica Clerk

Illustrated by Laura Rankin

Arthur A. Levine Books · An Imprint of Scholastic Press

All rights reserved. Published
by Scholastic Press, a division
of Scholastic Inc., Publishers
since 1920. SCHOLASTIC, SCHOLASTIC
PRESS and the LANTERN LOGO are
trademarks and/or registered
trademarks of Scholastic Inc.

No part of this publication may be reproduced,
or stored in a retrieval system, or transmitted in any
form or by any means, electronic, mechanical, photocopying,
recording, or otherwise, without written permission of the publisher.
For information regarding permission, write to Scholastic Inc., Attention:
Permissions Department, 557 Broadway, New York, NY 10012.

Library of Congress Cataloging-in-Publication Data
Clerk, Jessica.
The wriggly, wriggly baby / by Jessica Clerk; illustrated by Laura Rankin   p. cm.
Summary: A very active baby ventures from his home to the firehouse, the zoo,
the circus, and the beach, eluding his parents, until he finds himself alone
and discovers that he misses them.
ISBN 0-590-96067-9
[1. Babies—Fiction. 2. Stories in rhyme.] I. Rankin, Laura, ill. II. Title
PZ8.3.C558 Wr 2002   [E]--dc21   2001023527
1 3 5 7 9 10 8 6 4 2   02 03 04 05 06
Printed in Singapore   46
First edition, August 2002
The type was set in 21-point Dolores Bold.
The art for this book was created using ink and acrylics.
Book design by Kristina Albertson

For my parents
—J. C.

For baby Josh,
with love
—L. R.

Once there was a baby who wriggled real bad.

His mama tried to kiss him but it made him so mad;

his daddy went to hug him but he twisted away.
He just wriggled, wiggled, scriggled all night and all day.

When Granny came to see him he was cooing in his chair; she leaned to pat his chin . . . but that baby wasn't there!

The cat purred and pounced, but he didn't stop to play, oh!
The dog barked so loud, but *that* baby didn't stay. No!

He slithered down the banister; he inched across the floor, waved good-bye to the parrot . . .

and skittered out the door.

He skeetered down the walk, and he squiggled up the street,

and that scriggly, giggly baby
clapped his hands and tapped his feet.

To the firehouse he sauntered, turned a somersault or two,

pitter-pattered through the park, ziggle-zaggled to the zoo.

There he tangoed with the tigers, and he babbled to the bears.

The elephants applauded when he back-flipped up *the* stairs.

For the penguins he did pirouettes; he yodeled for the yak

and chatted with a crocodile who chitter-chattered back.

"Stay!" cried all *the* tigers
when he teetered through *the* gate
and *tottered to the diner*—

how that hungry baby ate!!!

He finished every special from *the* blue plate *to* the green,
half-a-dozen cherry pies, and a purple jellybean.

He sang for his supper; every diner shouted "More!"
But while those diners shouted . . . he skedaddled out the door.

Through the city to the circus, from the circus to the fair,

every place his parents looked, why, *their baby wasn't there!*

To the beach that baby bobbled, then he shimmied to the sea, and he waltzed when the whales hummed a briny symphony.

He waltzed and he wriggled till the whales went to sleep, sinking slowly to their beds far out in the deep.

Then he whistled for the stars and he wiggled for the moon, but clouds came and covered up her round face soon.

And when *that* wiggly, scriggly baby was left all alone,

he missed his mama and his daddy . . .

and he wriggled on home.